My First
Christmas

My First Christmas

Kim Ward

To order additional copies of this book, contact:
Xlibris
800-056-3182
www.Xlibrispublishing.co.uk
Orders@Xlibrispublishing.co.uk
741826

CONTENTS

Dedicated to Lexi Demi Collins

CHAPTER ONE

The Christmas Tree

I had become used to life with my forever family; even if I did have to go to the vets! Everyone was different. Mum used a stick in the house, dad had cerebral palsy and was always falling over, the other lady had learning difficulties and the boy was always playing loud music. It was lovely to be with so many nice people.

What's your human family like?

Kim Ward

Draw a picture of your family.

Even though I was so happy there was something else I really wanted. I really wished I could go out in the world that I could see from the windows. There were trees, leaves, bushes, mud, people and best of all, lots of other cats to talk to.

What can you see from your window?

Mum kept telling me it wasn't time yet and I really didn't know why!

Then one evening in December the whole house changed. It made me feel very unsettled and very, very scared.

Do you ever feel like that?

The boy climbed up a long ladder and got something very strange and new to me, out of the loft. I had seen them out of the window, but not in the house. I thought to myself 'Why do they want one of those in the house?'

Do you know what it was?

Then he got a very big box and put it on the floor. When mum opened the box there was all this long glittery, shiny stuff in all sorts of colours; Red, silver, gold and purple.

Do you know what it was?

It was tinsel.

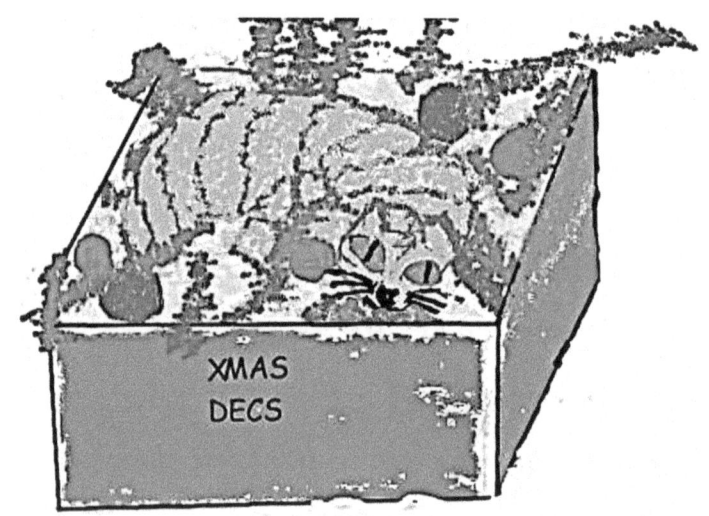

I couldn't resist it. I just had to dive in the box. I was swimming in an ocean of colours. It was just like a rainbow in a box.

I dug my paws deep down and found something else. Shiny, round things just like glittery balls. They were all sorts of colours. What had I found?

What is your favourite colour?

I felt like this was the best place on earth. I was fighting with the tinsel and kicking the baubles around. It was fantastic.

Then the human dad put the green thing on a stand, on the carpet. They called it a Christmas tree. That's what it was! This was the first time I had seen a Christmas tree. Mum began taking the tinsel out of the box and putting it on the Christmas tree.

I was upset. All I wanted to do was play with all the shiny things. I grabbed the end of the tinsel and tried pulling it back into the box. Mum was trying to put them on the Christmas tree.

Do you know why tinsel and baubles might be bad for animals?

Then mum was taking the baubles out of the box. It wasn't fair; I wanted to play with the tinsel and baubles. "If you break one it will cut you. They are as sharp as glass," mum said to me.

Mum was a lot stronger than me and pulled them away from me saying, "NO Pickles it's bad for animals! You might chew it and be ill, or get it caught around you and hurt yourself!"

I didn't understand what she meant.
Do you?

It wasn't long before mum was winning. There was more tinsel and baubles on the tree than in the box. It wasn't fair. I felt sad and I didn't want to be in the box anymore. I jumped out.

I was so sad I wanted to run away and be out in the world I could see through the window.

What do you do when you are upset?

The human family stepped back and all agreed that the Christmas tree looked lovely.

Do you help decorate your Christmas tree?

Draw your Christmas tree here.

CHAPTER TWO

The Plan

That night I made a plan!!

When all the humans were asleep I jumped on to the chair, climbed up the curtains and tried to squeeze out of a tiny window. I thought I was being so clever. I had squeezed my head and front paws through the tiny window. But I didn't feel so clever when I realised I was stuck!

Half of me was out of the window I could smell the outside world 'FREEDOM' I thought.

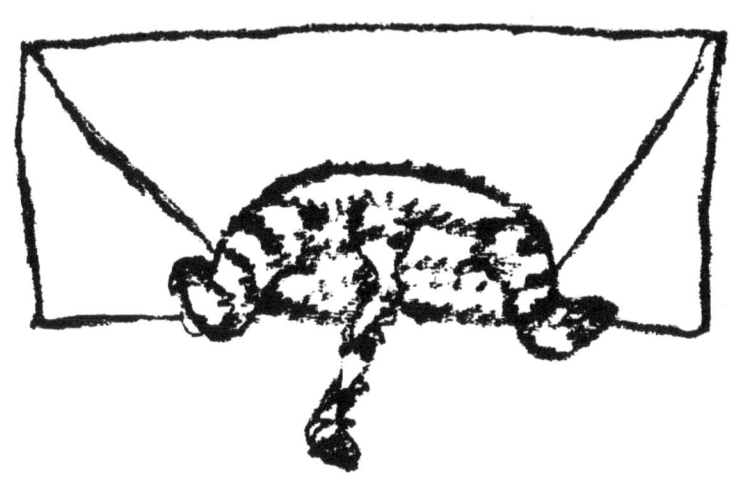

I wasn't so free. The back half of me was stuck on the curtain. I struggled and struggled. It was no good I had to call for help.

By now I was very, very scared. "MEOW, MEOW, MEOWWWWWWWW." My meows got louder and louder. Finally mum woke up.

She wasn't happy with me. She woke the human dad and boy. The dad went out into the front garden in his dressing gown and was trying to push me back in. The boy was in the living room trying to pull me in.

I thought it was very funny, but I knew the humans weren't happy with me. Mum was shouting at me.

Do you try to do naughty things and get into trouble for it?

So there I was stuck, half in and half out. I felt very silly and thought I would be stuck forever.

After a few minutes of me feeling very scared the boy climbed on the chair and he grabbed me by my back legs and pulled. I screeched and hissed. "That hurt."

"You silly thing!" the boy said to me.

I jumped out of his arms and ran to my mum. My heart was pounding and I really needed a cuddle.

"You are naughty!" she said. Then she gave me a cuddle. "After your injections tomorrow you will be able to go out in the garden and we will teach you where you live."

Little did the family know what I had planned for the next day!!

I bet you can't guess what I was going to do!!

CHAPTER THREE

The house gets decoRated

That morning all the humans went out and I was in the house on my own. Well I got straight to work. I didn't think about what I was doing and that it might be naughty.

I reached up and pulled the tinsel off the bottom of the tree. That was all I could reach. I was dragging it all around the living room and kitchen. I was getting wrapped up in tinsel and the kitchen was getting decorated.

I was having so much fun, that I went back to the tree for some more tinsel.

This time I decorated the sofa with it. There were tiny bits of glittery colour all over the place. I went back to the tree and pulled off the baubles that I could reach.

I kicked them and rolled them around. Some went under the sofa. So I went back to get more from the tree. By the time I had finished the bottom of the tree was empty.

I was really pleased with myself, but at the same time I knew it was wrong. I didn't know what to do.......

What would you do?

I felt scared, so I curled up on the armchair and went to sleep.

Soon the noise of angry humans woke me up. They were not happy with me.

I looked at them all cute as if to say "Wasn't me!"

It didn't work I was put in my cat carrier, so the family could clean up. It's a bit like you having time out on the naughty step.

It felt like I was in the box for hours. I was bored and hungry. Once it was all cleared up they let me out again, but I went and hid under the desk. I knew I had been bad and I was sulking.

Do you sulk when you get told off?

At bed time I curled up with mum to say sorry and we had a nice cuddle. Then I went to sleep on her head. It was a nice end to a bad day.

CHAPTER FOUR

The Needle

The next morning after breakfast mum put me in my cat carrier again. I thought they didn't love me anymore and didn't want me.

Do you ever feel like that?

This was the first time I really thought my family were giving me away.

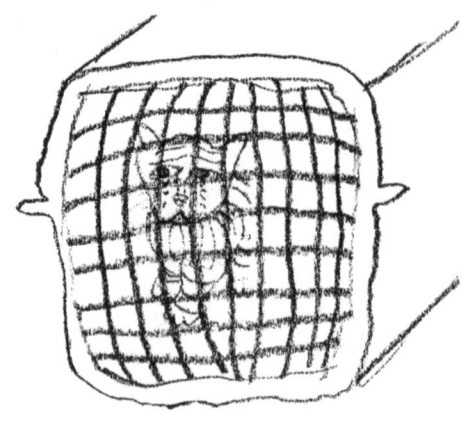

Although I felt like crying out loud I was really good in the car.

I wanted to make mum happy.

When the car stopped we were at the vets again. "OH NO!!!!" I thought to myself.

The vet weighed me and he was happy that I had put on a little bit of weight. Do you know anyone who has problems with their weight?

Some humans don't eat enough and get unwell.

Does the doctor weigh you?

He checked me all over. Then I saw the needle! My heart was pounding, I wanted to escape, but there was nowhere to go. So I pushed my head against mum.

"MEOOOWWWWWW!" I screamed and got back in the box. "I won't be naughty again I promise!" I meowed.

"Let him sleep it off today, then tomorrow begin taking him out on his harness and lead." The vet told mum.

When we got home I didn't want my dinner. I drank some water then went to sleep on the comfy sofa. When mum went to bed I got on her head and felt safe with my mum.

What makes you feel safe?

CHAPTER FIVE

SNOW

The next morning something really strange happened. I looked out of the window. Where had the ground gone? Everything was white.

Do you know what had happened?

Mum said it has been snowing, but it was still alright for me to learn how to go out in the garden. She put this fabric thing around my body and then she put a long cord thing on to it.

I was wearing a harness and lead. "What's going on I thought to myself?"

This was the first time mum had put it on me.

Mum picked me up and she opened a door I hadn't been through before. She said it was the back door.

Mum put me down on the cold wet ground. I lifted one of my front paws and shook it. It was freezing cold. I lifted my other front paw and shook that. I didn't like it.

This was my first time in the garden.

I didn't like this thing called snow. Mum picked me up and we went back in doors. I was shaking, so much, mum cuddled me; and then I was lovely and cosy.

I had some cat biscuits then curled up on the chair for a nap. If that was how the world outside the window felt I really didn't want to go out in it.

Later that day the snow had started melting and soon all the white was gone. Mum put my harness and lead on me again and we went outside. This time it was different. I could feel the cold, wet grass under my feet. This was the first time I had felt grass under my feet. The wetness felt funny on my paws, I was only used to the carpet and floor in the house.

I sniffed the fresh air and it smelt different from the house. I could smell the scents of other animals and saw the dark grey sky. I slowly moved one paw then another one. It took me a few minutes to get used to walking on the grass. Then I was running and jumping and rolling around. I really liked the garden. I licked the wet grass, I drank the melted snow. All I could taste was dirty, cold water. It was horrible.

Soon we had to go back in doors. It was hard work learning about new things around me. Smells, tastes and sounds were all new to me.

Over the next few days mum took me out in the garden on my lead. Each time I ventured a little bit further. I looked under the bushes, I dug the ground and I heard the meow of another young, male cat.

Who was he?

Every day I felt more confident being outside. I got use to the smells and sounds but I really wanted a friend to play with. Playing by myself was not fun.

Who do you play with?

Then one afternoon the boy put the harness and lead on me and we went out of the front door. It was very busy; cars people and noises. At first I was very scared and unsure. I looked at the boy, I didn't want to walk. It was my first time out in the street.

He said, "Come on you scaredy-cat!" He was right I was very scared. Then some lady humans walked up to us and started stroking me. "Oh isn't he lovely," they told the boy. Then he began to blush he always felt embarrassed around girls.

Soon I got up the courage to move very, very, very slowly. I sniffed everything as we went along. I smelt flowers, grass, pathways, and I even stopped to sniff the brick wall, the car tyres and everything I saw. This was all at a snail's pace. It must have taken us an hour to go the distance of three gardens.

Soon the boy was bored and we went home. That was enough for one day. I was tired and curled up on the chair.

It didn't take long for the boy to be more interested in taking me for walks because the girls would stop and talk to him. Within a few days we had gone all the way round the block and back. I felt really excited and ready to go out without my lead.

CHAPTER SIX

New fRiends

One day when mum took me out into the garden she took my lead off. It really surprised me. At first I froze. Then the curiosity in me took over. I moved a few steps, but looked back at my mum to make sure she was waiting for me. I felt safe knowing she was around. I took a few more steps and looked to check if mum was still there.

It was like my first day at school. I wanted to go exploring, but I needed to know mum would always be there for me.

What was your first day at school like?

I ventured a little further; suddenly I heard the meow of a young boy cat. He was in the garden next door. I was slow and cautious. I guess I was shy and felt scared at the thought of making new friends. It was the first time I met him.

Do you find it hard to make new friends?

Then the call of the other cat got the better of me and I went right over to the wooden fence, which divided the two gardens. I peered through a gap in the wood. I meowed softly. At first there was no reply.

Then mum called out "Sidney." A young, ginger and white cat leapt over the fence and made me jump. Who was Sidney? I thought. He came over to me and nudged his nose against me. I pulled away.

At the time I didn't know this was how cats greeted each other. It's like when grownups shake hands with someone they have just met. Children hug each other, or do a high five.

How do you greet new people you have just met?

I was very nervous, because Sidney was a lot bigger than me. He rubbed himself against my mum's legs and this made me feel jealous. She was my human, not his!

Mum stroked him, so I went towards her. I wanted to be friends with the cat but I really didn't understand cat language. I had a lot to learn.

Sidney came over to me to try and rub himself against me, but this frightened me, so I moved away. I really wasn't sure what friends do.

Each day mum took me out in the garden without my lead on. I was very happy rolling around in the grass, sniffing the plants, and looking for naughty things to do. Sometimes I would hide from mum and she would be calling for me.

"Pickles, where are you?" I would make her wait then jump out on her. I always made her jump.

It was like playing hide-and-seek in the playground.

Do you do that?

After the first day I often met Sidney in the garden. Soon we became very good friends. We would chase each other around the garden, play hide and seek, chase each other's tails. It was great fun. Sometimes Sidney went out of the garden, but I felt too scared to follow him.

CHAPTER SEVEN

ChRistMas day

Then on 25th December there was a lot going on. There was noise and brightly coloured, wrapped packages everywhere.

Do you know what day it was?

That's right it was Christmas day.

This was my first Christmas, so I really didn't know what was going to happen.

What do you do on Christmas day?

Some families don't celebrate Christmas.

Mum put me in my box and packed my bowls, cat biscuits and litter tray. Dad and the boy put all the presents Father Christmas had left for the family, in the car.

Where were we going? I thought.

Mum got in the car and put the cat box, with me in it, on her lap.

Dad drove the car. We were going a different way! I looked out of the car window, but I didn't recognise any of the buildings.

Dad parked the car in a big drive way. Mum got the cat box out of the car and carried me into a different house.

There were smells and voices that I knew; they had been to our house lots of times. I just didn't know this house.

Then I heard a man's voice. I knew him, he was a friend. He had visited our house and played with me. Mum let me out of the carrier. I just had to go exploring this new place.

I was running up and down the long hallway. Hiding under tables, playing hide and seek, leaping out on people and making them jump. It was great fun.

Suddenly when I went to jump up onto a small table, things started falling down on me!

Packets of crisps, bags of sweets, fruit and nuts; then the table cloth fell down and covered me. I was buried! I just lay there meowing.

What had I done?

Then I heard a lady's voice. I knew who she was. It's funny, but she was also called mum.

"He will have to go home!" she shouted. "I can't have everything ruined!"

My mum was in tears. She picked me up, cuddled me and said, "He's only a baby!"

"Well that's why I didn't let you have pets when you were Kids! They make too much mess!" The woman shouted.

I thought," Well she's not a very nice human."

Mum put me back in my carrier, got all my things together and we got in the car.

Dad drove us back home. Mum let me out of my carrier, put some lovely roast chicken and cat biscuits in my bowls, filled up my water.

Then she put my blanket on the floor in the kitchen. Mum gave me a cuddle and put me on the floor in the kitchen and walked away!

She calmly said, "I'm sorry little man, but you will have to spend the day on your own!" She closed the door.

Straight away I started crying for her. I heard her foot steps as she walked away. I could sense mum was not happy. I was her baby and she had to leave me all on my own, just because I pulled the table cloth. Then she closed the front door.

I felt so lonely! I cried and cried, but no one came back. It felt like hours before I finally cried myself to sleep on my blanket, which smelt of mum.

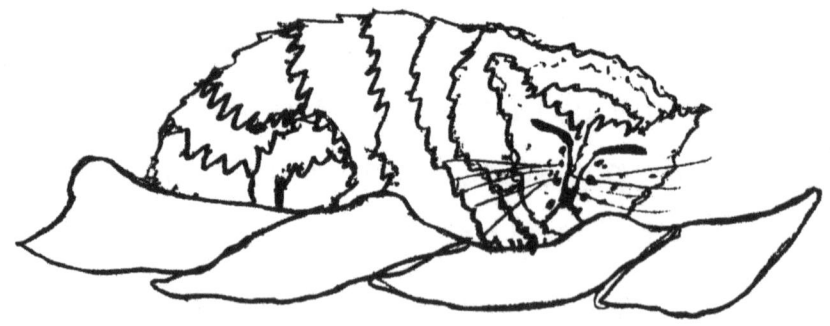

It wasn't nice being all on my own on Christmas day! Even if I didn't understand what Christmas day was all about.

Do you know anyone who spends Christmas on their own?

After a few hours I woke up and ate some of my chicken. I was feeling very sad, but no one was there for me.

Do you ever feel like that?

It was dark by the time the family came home. I was still crying and scratching on the kitchen door.

When mum opened the door, I was so happy to see everyone. I just couldn't keep still.

Mum gave me a very big cuddle and she whispered in my ear, "I will never do that to you again, little man."

I thought to myself, 'I'm going to get my own back on the woman who didn't want me there on Christmas day!'

CHAPTER EIGHT

The visitoRs

By now I was sleeping through the night, but still on mum's head. I didn't need mum to feed me I had learned how to crunch biscuits, lap water and most importantly chew chicken.

The next day I woke up on mum's head, we got up and she fed me. She had a cup of tea with the human dad. They didn't have time to cuddle me and play.

What was going on?

Had I been naughty?

Do you feel like that when people don't take any notice of you?

They were preparing food. Dad was peeling potatoes and carrots. Mum put a very big piece of meat in the oven to cook. I thought, 'I want some of that.' It all smelt very nice.

Then dad went out in the car and the boy was playing on his computer game, so I sat watching the meat cooking in the oven. I was feeling very hungry and licking my lips.

When the dad came home he had that horrible lady with him and the man who was friendly. Straight away I began thinking of how I could get her back for not letting me be with them on Christmas day.

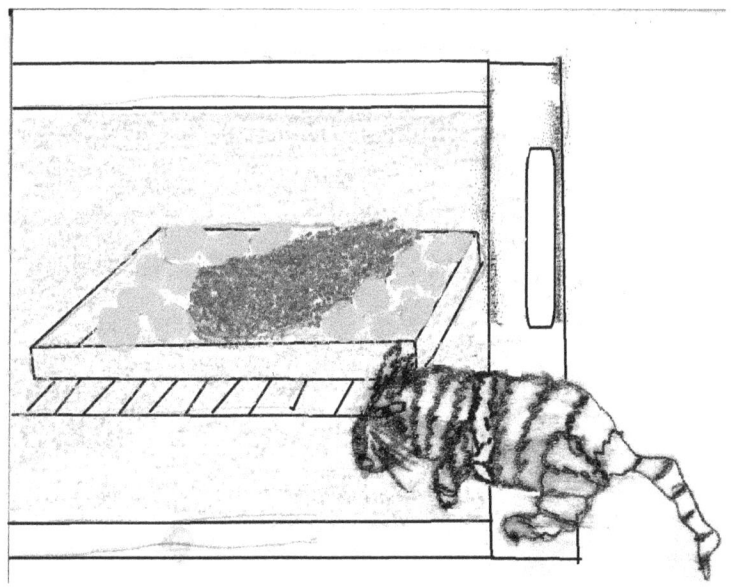

The man played with me, we always had rough play; which I really liked. It meant I didn't get told off for biting or scratching people. This is something cats do naturally, our wild instincts tell us to fight and catch prey.

I had forgotten all about the meat in the oven, until a smell came from the kitchen. It was lovely. I stopped playing and went into the kitchen.

"Not yet little man, it's too hot!" mum told me. So I sat and waited, and waited, and waited. Finally she had cut a small slice of the meat, cut it up and blown on it to cool it down.

Did your humans do that with your food when you were a baby?

Mum put the lovely, brown meat in my dinner bowl. I hadn't tasted anything this delicious before. I thought chicken was the best thing ever, but this was better. It was roast beef. Yum, Yum.

I woofed it down straight away and sat there waiting for more. Everyone was busy, so I was being ignored. I didn't like that, so I went and hid under the table.

Soon I smelt food again. Mum was dishing up. They had the lovely brown meat, roast potatoes, carrots, peas, sprouts and gravy.

All I was interested in was the meat. I sat by the dining table nicely waiting to be given some.

Then mum gave me a small piece. Dad followed with a bigger bit, and then the other man gave me a tiny piece.

I was working my way around the chairs. Lastly it was the horrible lady who didn't want me at her house. I really couldn't help myself. As she offered me a bit of meat I took it from her and bit her finger.

She yelled and I ran!

Everyone was shouting at me. I thought 'well she doesn't like me so why should I be nice to her?'

I know that it was very wrong of me.

What would you have done?

The lady was shouting at me and telling my mum that I was "A GREEDY ANIMAL!"

Well she was right I was an animal.

I was put in my cat carrier again, as punishment. I seem to spend a lot of time in my cat box.

Are you in time out a lot?

After dinner there was pudding. I smelt the cream and started wining. Mum let me out of the box and she whispered in my ear, "I know you don't like her and I don't blame you; but if you are going to be part of this family you have to be nice to everyone!"

Then mum put a tiny dish with an even smaller bit of cream in it. I lapped it up very quickly. Licked my lips and gave myself a good wash. Now it was time for a nap.

The horrible lady and the friendly man stayed a long time after dinner. Dad drove them home, while mum gave me a cuddle and watched the ten 'O' clock news.

When dad got back he told mum he didn't want me begging at the dinner table any more. Mum agreed to train me in a different way.

We all went to sleep and I knew I had been a bad boy, but I promised myself tomorrow would be a better day.

To be continued...........

A MESSAGE FROM PICKLES

I hope you have a very Happy Christmas and that you are good for your family.

We all have to learn the rules and sometimes we break them. But this is how we learn. I have made a lot of mistakes and find some rules hard to keep to. I have tested the boundaries, and been told off.

If you enjoyed my stories so far then let me know and tell your friends about them. picklespress@yahoo.co.uk or contact me on Facebook @picklespress

Remember that no one, human or animal, is purrfect. So just keep learning, don't give up and remember there is always someone you can talk to.

If you are being bullied, if you are lonely, if you worry about how you look, if you lose someone or your family changes.

Tell a teacher, a friend, a grown up you trust or contact me.

Email me at picklespress@yahoo.co.uk

I will always try to help.

I will get my human to read it to me and I will tell them what to write back to you.

Love from Pickles